Beto and the Bone Dance

Gina Freschet

FARRAR STRAUS GIROUX

NEW YORK

This one's for Steve

Copyright © 2001 by Gina Freschet

All rights reserved

Distributed in Canada by Douglas & McIntyre Ltd.

Color separations by Hong Kong Scanner Arts

Printed in the United States of America by Worzalla

Typography by Judy Lanfredi

First edition, 2001

1 3 5 7 9 10 8 6 4 2

Library of Congress Cataloging-in-Publication Data

Freschet, Gina.

Beto and the bone dance / Gina Freschet.— 1st ed.

p. cm.

Summary: Beto searches all day for something all his own to put on his grandmother's grave for the Day of the Dead.

ISBN 0-374-31720-8

[1. All Souls' Day—Fiction. 2. Mexican Americans—Fiction.] I. Title.

PZ7.F889685 Be 2001

[E]—dc21

00-44287

A Glossary of Spanish Words and Phrases in This Book

abuela: grandmother

calabaza: pumpkin or squash

calavera: skull

centro: town center

diablo: devil

el Día de los Muertos: the Day of the Dead

gracioso: funny

Lo siento: I'm sorry

mariachi: street musician

¡Mira!: Look!

pan de muertos: bread of the dead

panteón: cemetery

refresco: soda pop

tamarindo: tamarind, a kind of fruit

tía: aunt

tío: uncle

tumba: grave

¡Uno, dos!: One, two!

vela: candle

zonzo: fool

The skeletons have started to appear. In shop windows, on balconies, in houses—skeletons all over town.

Beto laughs at all the skulls. He loves these crazy *calaveras*. They're loco!

This is his favorite holiday. In many places it's called Halloween. But here it's *el Día de los Muertos*. The Day of the Dead.

And one of Beto's favorite things about *el Día de los Muertos* is all the skeletons. So many kinds! Candy skeletons, ballerina skeletons. Skeletons at the beach, skeletons at the dentist, skeletons playing the marimba.

"*¡Mira!* Poppy—look!" says Beto. *"Gracioso."*

"Very silly," Poppy agrees. "Keep poking fun at them to show them we're not afraid."

"We're not scared of you *zonzos*!" hoots Beto.

Poppy takes Beto through town to see all the altars made this year. Every shop and home and little square has one. Lacy paper cutouts rustle from them like banana leaves.

Each altar is made in memory of someone who died. But today isn't a sad time. Just the opposite. *El Día de los Muertos* is a day for celebration.

The altars hold all the dead person's favorite foods and treats and toys. This is to welcome them home for one night a year.

Beto and Poppy are making an altar for Beto's *abuela*—his grandmother who died last spring. First, they must go to the market.

Poppy inspects the *calabazas*. Beto gets to pick out the flowers. Later, their relatives will come to help decorate the altar. Beto wants to add something all his own to the altar—something Abuela will know is just from him.

The market bursts with fruits and flowers. Clouds of incense float by, and skulls stare with tinfoil eyes.

Beto looks up at the beeswax candles hanging overhead and says, "I know—I will bring those shiny striped *velas*."

"Sorry, Beto, but Tía Tish is bringing the *velas*," says Poppy.

They stop in front of the rows of *pan de muertos*, the bread of the dead. Beto sees one adorned with Abuela's favorite flower. "Then I'll bring that bread."

"*Lo siento*—sorry again," says Poppy, "but your cousins are already bringing the *pan de muertos*."

Beto frowns. He has to think of something else. And nothing seems right.

Back at home, Beto and Poppy set up the altar carefully. Beto fills the house with marigolds and purple cockscomb. At the table he makes figurines out of paper, with garbanzo-bean heads. Meanwhile, Poppy carves the *calabazas*.

"Make one look like Abuela," says Beto. "With big eyes and little teeth."

All the altars are filled with flowers and fruit. But there are personal decorations that make each one different.

Late that afternoon, Tía Tish and Tío Lolo arrive with Beto's
cousins Lety and Carmella.

Tía Tish arranges the candles she's brought and lights them.

Lety and Mella put their loaves of *pan de muertos* on the altar.

Beto racks his brain. Then he blurts, "I know! Abuela loved
soda pop." And he runs to get a *refresco*—Supra Fizzy, his favorite
kind.

But when he returns, Tío Lolo is already putting a bottle of *refresco* on the altar.

"I know," thinks Beto. "Abuela loved chocolate, too." And he runs to get some. But when he comes back, Mella has beat him to it.

Then Lety spreads out a whole bagful of nuts and grapes, candy *calaveras* and oranges, a pot of *tamarindo* chili, a scarf, a pin, and the cat's sequined collar. "This is all for Abuela," she announces.

Beto is flabbergasted. He runs and rummages in a closet. He comes back with an old shoe. Tía Tish clucks, "You don't put a shoe on the altar, Beto. What does that mean to your *abuela*?" And everyone looks at him.

Poppy tells him, "Help me put out the toy *mariachis*. Your *abuela* loved music." But Beto wants to add something all his own.

He goes outside and kicks at the dirt in order to think. He sulks at the setting sun.

Soon it's night. Beto and his family gather up flowers and candles to make a little altar at the *panteón*—the cemetery. Tonight Beto's allowed to stay up all night long.

In the *centro* fireworks spit. The streets are filled with people, some of them disguised as *diablos* and superheroes. Beto and his family join a procession of spooks and musicians who troop from house to house, singing loud for bread and chocolate.

Soon Beto has a foamy chocolate mustache.

At last they come to the *panteón*.
Beto holds his breath as he enters
the big gates. The *panteón* is lit up
with the flames of a thousand *velas*
and filled with fountains of flowers.

Lots of people are already there. Musicians stroll and sing and play guitars. There is the smell of burning incense and scorched marigold blossoms. Families picnic on the decorated graves of their ancestors. They tell stories and laugh and remember all the good things the person did while alive.

Tía Tish puts Abuela's favorite dishes on the *tumba*—the grave.
Lety and Mella play checkers and dice on the stone.

Beto sprinkles marigold petals around the *tumba*. "So Abuela
can find her way here," he says.

"At midnight," Tía Tish says, "the spirits will come out to visit.
They will take the flavor from the food we've left for them."

Thinking about the spirits gives Beto the willies. Will they know he sneaked a lick of one of the sugar *calaveras*? Will he be in trouble for putting a shoe on Abuela's altar? He shivers, and Mella teases him for having chicken skin.

The church bells sound eleven low gongs and the stars shiver, too. Beto gets sleepy trying to count them, and he has to close his eyes.

Then there is a sound like dry sticks on paper drums, and Beto sits up.

Clickety-clackety bump!

"Uh-oh!" says Beto. He reminds himself that he's not afraid of those crazy *calavera* clowns. But he is, just a little.

Until, all in a chorus, the skeletons jump out.

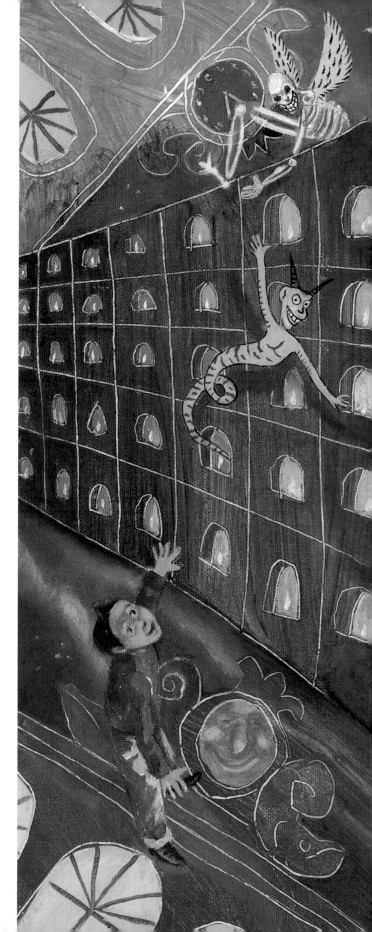

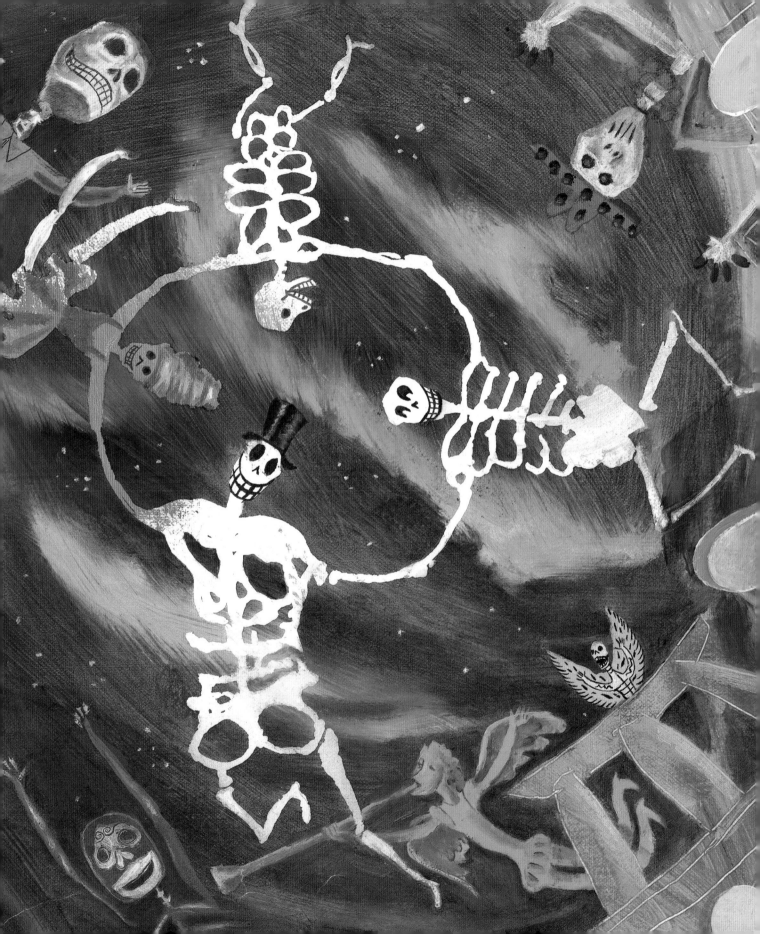

"They're doing a bone dance!" shouts Beto.

And so they are. The skeletons dance and clack their jaws and sing:

> "Tonight we get to leave our beds
> and crack our knuckles, knock our heads.
> We dance the salsa and the cha-cha,
> do the tango and the conga!"

Beto laughs. A friendly skeleton pulls him into the dance. In no time Beto's singing, "¡Uno, dos, cha-cha-cha!"

"*Bump your hipbones, bump your shins,*
fling your ribs like bowling pins."

They do the Calavera Cakewalk, the Skeleton Stomp,
and the Bony Maroney.

"Snap your fingers, click your thumbs,
bang your kneecaps like two drums!"

They dance the Halloween Hula, the Monster
Mambo, and the Tibia Twist.

Beto calls out, "Follow me." And he leads all the skeletons in a conga line.

The bone dance is so much fun that Beto looks for his family to join in. But he can't find them. In that moment he's all alone, with nothing but bones.

He feels a chill in his own bones.
Then he sees someone he knows.

"Abuela!" Beto runs to his grandmother, who holds him in arms as soft as braided bread. "Oh, Abuela, I'm sorry," he says. "I couldn't find anything you loved to put on your altar."

"Hush, little one," says Abuela. "I'll tell you what I love most of all."

Suddenly Beto isn't in Abuela's arms anymore. Poppy is holding him instead, whispering, "Beto, wake up. It's midnight."

"Can you feel the spirits?" asks Tía Tish. "They're all among us, like the wind."

Beto says, "I know, I know!" He fishes in Poppy's pocket.

"What are you looking for?" Poppy asks.

Beto finds Poppy's wallet and takes out a small snapshot. "This is what Abuela wants on the altar." It's a picture of Beto.

"It's true," says Poppy. "She loved you most of all."

Beto places his photo among the marigolds on the *tumba*.

The family tell wonderful stories about Abuela all night long.